I'd like to dedicate this book to my students at the Loft Literary Center, to Camp Foley, and to all who love telling scary stories around a campfire.

TRUTH OR DARE

MIDNIGHT
TRUTH OR DARE

K.R. COLEMAN

darby creek
MINNEAPOLIS

Darby Creek
A division of Lerner Publishing Group, Inc.
241 First Avenue North
Minneapolis, MN 55401 USA

For reading levels and more information, look up this title at
www.lernerbooks.com.

Photos in this book used with the permission of: © iStockphoto.com/RonBailey (man with axe); © Pikoso.kz/Shutterstock.com (campfire); backgrounds: © iStockphoto.com/AF-studio, © iStockphoto.com/blackred, © iStockphoto.com/Adam Smigielski.

Main body text set in Janson Text LT Std 12/17.5.
Typeface provided by Adobe Systems.

Library of Congress Cataloging-in-Publication Data

Names: Coleman, K. R., author.
Title: Truth or dare / K. R. Coleman.
Description: Minneapolis : Darby Creek, [2017] | Series: Midnight | Summary: Recent graduates of Middleton High test their bravery in the woods where other young people have disappeared, and when one of their friends leaves the group and doesn't come back, they become increasingly scared.
Identifiers: LCCN 2016029180 (print) | LCCN 2016040726 (ebook) | ISBN 9781512427684 (lb : alk. paper) | ISBN 9781512430981 (pb : alk. paper) | ISBN 9781512427882 (eb pdf)
Subjects: | CYAC: Truth or dare (Game)—Fiction. | Missing persons—Fiction. | Forests and forestry—Fiction. | Courage—Fiction. | Fear—Fiction.
Classification: LCC PZ7.1.C644 Tr 2017 (print) | LCC PZ7.1.C644 (ebook) | DDC [Fic]—dc23

LC record available at https://lccn.loc.gov/2016029180

Manufactured in the United States of America
1-41493-23354-9/7/2016

CHAPTER 1

It is hot for early June. The air hangs humid
and heavy. Trey shoots a basketball and mutters
to himself, "Dominic, where *are* you?" They're
supposed to be leaving for the weekend—camping
out to celebrate their graduation—and Trey can't
wait to get away from Middleton. Dominic lives
just a few blocks away, and Trey can see his blue-
and-white rambler from here, but not his car. They
were supposed to leave an hour ago.

He has just pulled out his phone to send
another text when he hears the catlike yowl of
Dominic's car turning the corner. The power
steering went out years ago, but Dominic insists it
is fine to drive—it just takes a little extra muscle to
crank the wheel.

The rusty blue Buick pulls into the driveway, and Trey sees someone else sitting in the front seat: Willa McBride, Dominic's ex-girlfriend. *Wait, is she coming with us?* he wonders. He was hoping for a relaxing, drama-free weekend of sitting around and fishing. He's been working extra shifts at the restaurant his parents own, and this is his first weekend off in months.

"Hey," Dominic says as he gets out of the car. He's wearing jeans, an old T-shirt, and an Arizona State baseball hat.

"Are you two back together?" Trey says, glancing at the car and then tossing Dominic the basketball. Six months ago Dominic and Willa broke up, then they got back together, and then they broke up again. Trey had to deal with them both, and he'd never been so annoyed with two people in his life.

"We're just friends," Dominic says, bouncing the ball. "But I want to hang out with her before I leave—and this is it. On Monday I'm out of here, and I don't know when I'll be back."

Dominic does a smooth layup. He's shorter than Trey, but he's always been the better athlete—quicker, faster, more determined. He's off to play baseball for Arizona State. The coach wants him to start training on Monday.

Trey knows how hard Dominic worked to catch the eye of a scout, but he can't imagine what it will be like without him. Every day for the past three years they've driven to school and baseball practice together in that blue Buick—windows down, music cranked up, making plans to get out of Middleton and see the world.

Willa gets out of the car and pulls her dark, curly hair up into a bun on top of her head.

"Maybe you two should just go," Trey says, nodding at Willa. He doesn't want to end up being the third wheel on this camping trip. "My folks could use my help. I'm leaving them short-staffed this weekend."

"Come on," Dominic says as he passes the ball to Trey. "They'll be fine without you, and besides, they'll have to get used to you not being around when you leave in the fall."

Trey keeps his face neutral. He isn't leaving Middleton. Money is really tight for his family right now. The restaurant is barely breaking even, so he's decided to put off college for another year.

He hasn't told Dominic this; he hasn't told anyone yet. A part of him wants to believe that things will work out and he'll be able to head off to Madison at the end of August, but he can't leave while his parents are struggling.

Willa holds up her hands. Trey passes her the ball. She bounces it twice and then takes a shot. Despite the weird angle from where she is standing, the ball goes in.

Swish.

Focused and confident, Willa makes everything look effortless. She was their school's valedictorian and class president and was voted "most likely to succeed." She earned a full ride to Michigan State. Trey wishes he would've worked harder in school or pushed himself more in sports. A scholarship could've really helped him out.

"Let's get going," Dominic says. "The wilderness calls." He puts his hands around his mouth and makes the call of some kind of dying animal. Willa rolls her eyes, and Trey shakes his head.

Suddenly, the wind picks up. Sand and dust swirl around on the driveway, and dark clouds move in from the west.

"It doesn't look like good camping weather," Trey says.

Willa checks the weather on her phone and says, "It's just a passing storm. We'll be fine."

But Trey doesn't feel like things will be fine. The air smells like copper pennies—the scent of electricity and rain. This storm will be big.

"We can always turn around and head back home if we have to," Dominic says, also looking at the sky. "Lake Helen is just an hour away."

"What?" Trey says, looking at Dominic. "I thought the plan was to camp at Johnson National Park. That's where the fishing is good."

"Too far away," Willa says.

"I have get back early on Sunday to pack," Dominic says.

"Lake Helen?" Trey shakes his head. "Isn't that the place where that college student went missing a year ago?"

"I remember all the posters up around town," Willa says.

"We still have one up in the restaurant," Trey says.

"The kid isn't missing," Dominic says. "He took off. He was here on a student visa and didn't want to return to Russia."

Trey remembers watching the kid's mother talking to reporters on the news. She refused to believe her son had defected, but witnesses claimed they saw someone matching the kid's description getting on a bus to New York, and a grainy video confirmed the story.

Sasha, Trey remembers. That was the kid's name—Alexander, but his mother called him Sasha. It was written in bold, black ink on the poster near the front door of the restaurant.

A light rain begins to fall as Trey arranges his gear in the trunk of the car. There's another tent in there, a fishing pole, a baseball glove, and two other backpacks, but no sign of food of any kind. He pops his head out of the trunk. "I thought you said you were getting all the food."

"Leslie's bringing it," Dominic says.

"Leslie Miller?" Trey says. "She's coming too?"

Willa reaches past Trey into the trunk to grab a red raincoat out of her backpack.

"She's never been to Lake Helen, and she really wanted to go," Willa says, holding the jacket over her head. "Besides, her dad owns Middleton Grocery now, so she got all the food for free."

"Did you give her the list?" Trey says to Dominic. "Hot dogs? S'mores? Jiffy Pop? Tang?" That's what they got when they were younger, when they used to camp out in Dominic's yard.

Dominic shakes his head and slides into the driver's seat. "I'm sure she'll get plenty of good things to eat."

Willa gives him a flinty smile. "You don't know Leslie, do you?" She heads toward the front passenger seat, jumps in, and shouts, "Shotgun!"

Trey climbs in the backseat as Dominic and Willa laugh about something up front. As they drive away from his house, he wonders what other surprises await.

CHAPTER 2

Leslie Miller's house is a huge brick mansion at the top of a steep driveway. Trey knows there is a pool in back, but he's never been invited there to swim. Leslie's father owns half the town, including the strip mall where Trey's parents run their restaurant.

Over the past two years, Mr. Miller has increased his parents' rent so much that they can barely break even. Trey has been slipping more than half of his tips back in the till to try to help out. His parents really need to own their own building, but there isn't a place in town that they can afford right now. Mr. Miller has snapped everything up.

Leslie is waiting for them on the front

porch, her long brown hair blowing wildly around her face. Dominic hops out and opens the trunk while Trey helps Leslie with the cooler of food. The sky is darker, and the rain blows sideways in the wind.

"Maybe we should just hang out here until the storm passes," Trey says as they get into the backseat.

"No way," Leslie replies. "We need to leave before my dad gets back. He'd freak out if he knew I was spending the night at Lake Helen." She tucks her damp hair behind her ears and looks out the window. "He's never allowed me to go there my entire life."

"Even for the day?" Willa asks.

"He's convinced I'd get kidnapped or something. A friend of his went missing there a long time ago. She stepped into the woods just after midnight and was never seen again."

"When?" Trey says looking at her.

"Back in 1984."

"So that makes two people who disappeared there."

"Three," Leslie corrects him.

"Three?" Willa asks.

"A year after my dad's friend went missing, her sister went missing too."

"From Lake Helen?" Trey says.

Leslie nods. "I'll tell you about it around the campfire tonight. It is a long, weird story."

At the bottom of the driveway, the car splashes through a large puddle and howls as it turns onto the street.

"Do you think it is safe to camp there?" Willa says.

"We'll be fine," Leslie says, looking out her window. "The police concluded that the sisters ran away, but my dad is convinced someone or something lurks in the woods."

Dominic makes a ghostly *whoooo* sound as they turn onto the highway and drive west, straight into the storm.

CHAPTER 3

As they near Lake Helen, the rain falls so hard that the windshield wipers can't keep up. Trey watches Dominic grip the steering wheel and lean forward, trying to see the road ahead.

"You should just pull over," Trey says.

"We're almost there," Dominic replies, though he slows down. Up ahead, blurry brake lights glow red. "I think the turnoff is in less than a mile."

Trey leans forward in his seat too, looking for the sign. "I think that's the turn. Right here." He points to a green sign that is there and then gone.

Lightning flashes across the sky and thunder booms, and a gravel road appears to the right, marked with a faded wooden sign that says *Lake Helen*. It's small, as if no one wants anyone to find the place.

"Right here," Trey says. Dominic slams on the brakes, and they skid across the blacktop onto the muddy gravel road.

"Good eyes," Dominic says.

They drive up a steep, curvy hill. A thick, dark forest of massive pine trees looms to the left, and a grassy meadow opens on the right. Trey visited Lake Helen once before, back in sixth grade for a field trip, but nothing about the place seems familiar. The woods seem darker and more ominous.

Suddenly Willa yells, "Watch out!" Just in front of them, down the hill, a giant pine tree has fallen across the road. The car swerves and slides, and the seatbelt digs into Trey's stomach and chest as they go off the road and skid to a halt in a muddy ditch.

"Whoa," Dominic says, still gripping the wheel. "I did not see that."

"How could you not see a giant tree?" Willa says, glaring at him.

Thunder rumbles, and there's another flash of lightning.

No one seems hurt, but when Trey looks out his window, he sees the water in the ditch rising rapidly.

"We need to get out of here," Trey says.

Dominic steps on the gas, but the front wheels just spin.

"Put it in reverse." Trey looks out the back window. Dominic floors it, and the wheels throw up a fountain of muddy water, but the car stays put.

"Hold on." Trey jumps out of the car. The rain is cold and hard against his skin. As he breaks boughs off the fallen tree, he feels like someone is watching him from the woods. Another streak of lightning flashes in the sky, and something moves between two trees. Then it disappears. He hopes it isn't a bear—though at this point, he wouldn't be surprised if it was. Maybe they can just turn around and head back to Middleton as soon as they get the car out of the ditch.

Trey places the pine branches under the front and back wheels.

"Put it in drive," he says to Dominic, who has rolled his window down. "Ease the car forward.

Leslie sticks her head out the window. "Do you want us to get out and push?"

"No, I think this will do the trick," Trey says.

Dominic puts the car in drive, and the tires crunch against the pine branches.

"Steady," Trey says. "Now gun it."

The car lurches forward up the grassy, muddy bank and back onto the road, just on the other side of the fallen tree. Trey climbs out of the ditch, his shoes covered with mud and his clothes soaked through. As he makes his way to the car, he hears a slow and steady chopping sound coming from deep in the woods. *Who would be out cutting down a tree during a thunderstorm?*

Shivering, Trey looks back at the giant tree now behind him. He'd assumed the storm blew it down but now sees that it has been chopped off at the base.

"Well, I guess we're not turning back," Dominic says as Trey gets into the car.

"The tree was felled," Trey says.

"What?" Dominic says.

"Someone cut it down."

"Are you sure?"

"Go look for yourself."

"That's bizarre," Leslie says, handing him her dry sweatshirt. "I guess someone didn't plan out the angle of the fall."

Trey shakes his head at the sweatshirt. No sense getting her stuff wet and dirty too. Instead he wipes his face on his arms, though he feels chilled.

"Turn up the heat," Leslie says. "Trey's cold."

"I'm fine," Trey says, but a shivery feeling runs through his veins, a feeling that Lake Helen isn't where they should be.

As they drive toward the lake, the rain begins to let up.

"Look at that," Dominic says a mile down the road. "What did I tell you? It was just a passing storm. The sun is even starting to come out again." He turns off the windshield wipers and the lake comes into view, aquamarine water standing out against the black cliffs and evergreens.

They drive into the campground, and Trey thinks how strange it is that there is no one else there on a Saturday in June. Not one tent. Not one other car.

CHAPTER 4

Dominic pulls into the campsite closest to the lake.

"Prime real estate," Leslie says, getting out of the car and standing at the edge of the campsite. "Check out this lake view!"

"Let's head down there. It's still too wet to set up camp." Willa is already heading toward the lake, Leslie in tow.

"Don't you think it's weird no one else is here?" Trey says to Dominic as he pulls a dry shirt out of his backpack.

"I guess no one could get past that tree," Dominic says.

Something isn't right about this place, he thinks, but then he looks at the lake. The water is calm, reflecting the clear sky above, and the beach is covered with pinkish-white sand.

Leslie and Willa have already taken off their shoes and waded in. Trey and Dominic head down there and climb a large boulder at the edge of the lake.

Trey pitches a pebble into the water and watches a ring spread out across the lake, and then he looks at Dominic. "It is going to be so strange not going to school this fall."

"What are you talking about?" Dominic says. "You're heading off to Madison."

"I decided not to go. We just don't have the money." It felt good to confess it to someone.

"Man," Dominic says. "I'm sorry. I know how excited you were about going there."

Trey nods. He was excited. He was ready to get away. "I just can't leave. Not now. My parents are about to lose their restaurant, and I've got to figure out a way to help them."

"The food is amazing," Dominic says. "I don't understand why it isn't doing well."

Trey looks at Leslie down below. "The rent is too high. I think Leslie's dad is trying to run my parents out of the space."

Dominic slaps at a fly on his neck. "I know how much you wanted to get out of Middleton."

"Next year," Trey says as another fly buzzes around his head.

"Ow!" Dominic shouts, slapping at his shoulder. "Something just bit me."

A fly darts past Dominic's hand, and Trey sees blood where it bit through the fabric of his shirt.

More flies swarm around them, and Dominic and Trey swat wildly at their heads, necks, and arms. Off in the distance, Trey sees a black mass of flies descend on Leslie and Willa too.

"Ow! Ow! Ow!" the girls are shouting as they run from the lake, waving their hands and slapping at their faces and arms.

"Vampire flies!" Leslie yells as they race up the shore.

They flee back to the car. The flies follow and cling to the windows, trying to get in.

"Ugh. We can't camp here," Dominic says. There is a huge welt on the back of his neck and another behind his ear. "Those things are vicious." He starts up the car, and they drive down a narrow, bumpy road that circles the lake and then leads deeper into the woods.

"I don't think this is going to lead us back to the highway," Trey says after a few minutes.

"I don't care where it leads us, as long as we get away from those evil flies," Dominic says.

Trey and Leslie brace their hands against the ceiling of the car as they bounce around in the backseat. Trey has a vision of the rust bucket suddenly falling apart, wheels rolling off in different directions.

They cross a narrow wooden bridge, and on the other side is a small clearing and a ranger station. Dominic pulls up as close as he can to the building. Flies are swarming there too. Hundreds of them cling to the wooden siding. The air inside the car has become hot and stifling.

"On the count of three," Trey says, "we run to the building. One, two, three!" They jump out and run, but when they reach the building, the door is locked. They pull and pound on it as the flies descend, biting and buzzing.

They are about to run back to the car when a green ranger truck pulls up behind them. A tall, bearded man slowly gets out of the truck and ambles toward them as they swat at the flies and jump around.

"Move out of the way if you want in," the ranger says. There are flies in his beard and covering his tan ranger hat.

He unlocks the door, and the four of them pile into the shelter of the small, dark building. Trey smacks a black fly that is clinging to the back of his neck.

"What's the deal with the flies?" Leslie asks.

"The unusually hot and humid spring created the largest hatch I've ever seen," the ranger says with a smile. He shuts the door behind him and sits down at his desk. "Drove all the campers away."

A fly crawls around in the ranger's beard.

"How did they get past the tree?" Trey asks. "Is there another way out?"

The ranger pulls the fly from his beard. It struggles between his finger and thumb, wings beating furiously, and then he just lets it go. It circles his head once and attaches itself to the ceiling above, out of reach. Trey can't help but feel like it's staring down at all of them.

"That was a nearly two-hundred-year-old tree," the ranger says, scratching his beard. "Storm blew it down."

"No," Trey says, looking at him. Was the ranger intentionally ignoring his question? "It was cut down. I saw the marks."

"I had to do that," the ranger says, nodding and staring out the window across the room. "It came down partially, leaning against some trunks across the road, and I didn't want it to crush any cars that passed beneath. A crew won't be able to get out here until Monday."

Willa looks at the ranger and puts her hands on his desk. "There's no way we can camp here. We will go insane."

Dominic takes out his phone to call home.

"No reception here," the ranger says and then nods at the phone on his desk. "And the land lines are down because of the storm."

Leslie swats a fly on Willa's head.

"Ow," Willa says.

"What you kids can do is hike three miles up the trail and camp deeper in the woods. The flies like to stay near the lake. They won't follow you that far."

"Are you sure?" Dominic asks.

"Yeah, I'm sure," the ranger says as he takes a camping permit from a desk drawer.

"Your names?"

They give him their names, and he gives them the pink copy of the camping permit.

"Where you from?"

"Middleton," Willa says. "We just graduated."

He doesn't congratulate them. He doesn't look up. He just hands a map to Trey.

"You all have big plans for next year? Off to conquer the world?"

Trey looks down at the map. *This guy is strange*, he thinks. His eyes are a weird shade of green with a circle of amber around the iris. He's never seen eyes like that before.

"What about you?" the ranger asks, catching Trey off guard. "Where are you heading to this fall? What big plans have you made?"

It's like he knows I'm not going anywhere, he thinks, but out loud he just says, "I'm taking a year off."

Leslie and Willa turn toward him, startled, but the ranger just shrugs.

"Not a bad thing to do," he says. "'The world is too much with us; late and soon, getting and spending, we lay waste our powers.'"

"Wordsworth?" Willa asks.

"Very good," the ranger says. "A smart girl. A very smart girl."

A fly circles around and around them.

"You can go ahead and leave your car here. The trail starts at the end of this road," the ranger says, pointing to the door.

They make a run to the car, grab shirts out of their bags, and tie them around their heads to keep the flies off their faces. Then they shoulder their backpacks, divide up the food, and run for the woods.

The flies buzz and bite and follow them.

CHAPTER 5

"Why did we think this would be a good idea?" Dominic asks Trey as they run down the muddy trail, swatting at the swarming flies.

"We just need to keep going," Trey says.

The trail is wet and slippery, and it's hard to run without tripping over exposed rocks and gnarled roots. Welts mark Trey's arms and legs, and he can feel them on the back of his neck and scalp too. The other three look just as bad.

"What if he was lying to us?" Leslie says. "What if we all get eaten alive on this trail? Maybe that's what happened to those missing kids . . . the flies ate them. Not one piece of them left."

Ten minutes or so later, Trey slides to a

stop. Willa nearly collides with him.

"Do you hear that?" he says.

"What?" Leslie and Willa both say.

"The buzzing. It's gone."

They slowly unwrap the shirts from their heads. The biting flies have disappeared, and it is so quiet they can hear the wind rustle through the leaves.

"So. Much. Better," Willa declares, looking up at the tall trees surrounding them. "Ahh, peace. Quiet."

But the silence is broken by a distant but steady chopping sound.

"What is that?" Willa says.

They all stop and listen.

"Someone must be splitting logs or cutting down a tree," Trey says.

"Maybe it's the ranger trying to clear the tree on the road," Dominic says.

Trey faces the sound and realizes that it is coming from the direction opposite the road—from deep within the woods. Then the sound stops, and the forest is quiet again.

Too quiet, Trey thinks.

CHAPTER 6

A wooden sign bearing the words *Great Red Pine* appears, nailed to a post beside the trail. An arrow points up a path perpendicular to the main trail.

Trey pulls the permit—now damp with sweat as well as rain—from his pocket and checks it. "That's our campsite," he confirms.

They follow the path up a small hill, pushing low-hanging branches out of their way. It ends in a small clearing with a metal fire pit in the middle and enough space for two tents off to one side. A mat of pine needles covers the ground, and the evergreen smell rises as they drop their backpacks to explore.

"So hungry!" Leslie says. She digs in her bag and hands everyone a granola bar.

Suddenly starving, Trey opens his and takes a bite—but stops chewing when he discovers it tastes like sand.

"What is this?" he asks.

"A soy crunch bar," Leslie replies.

"Yum," Trey says, trying to wash it down with a swig of water. He thinks about big handfuls of fake-butter-flavored Jiffy Pop snagged from a tinfoil bubble and swigs of sugary orange soda as he chokes down the last bite.

"We should set up the tents," Willa says.

"Where are they?" Trey looks at the pile of backpacks, and his stomach sinks.

"I thought you grabbed them," Dominic says.

They all look at one another. Heavy, dark clouds are rolling across the tiny circle of sky visible from the camp.

"Rock, paper, scissors?" Leslie suggests. Soon she and Trey are grinning at the losers.

"Dominic, it looks like it's you and me, bud." Willa grabs a shirt to tie around her head.

"Rematch?" Dominic asks.

"You'll be fine," Trey says. "Just try and get back before dark."

"It isn't really that far of a walk," Willa says. "Come on. Trey's right. We don't want to have to hike back here in the dark."

"We'll have a fire going by the time you get back," Leslie volunteers as she digs in her pack for a book of matches.

Trey doesn't say anything. He just smiles as Dominic wraps a T-shirt around his neck and head. If it was just the two of them on this trip, Trey knows they would've forgotten about getting the tent and just slept under the stars.

"I'm going to search for some dry tinder," Leslie says. She heads for another trail, this one barely an opening in the trees, eyes already on the ground.

"I thought you said something about not entering the woods alone," Trey calls after her, but she just keeps going.

"After midnight," she says, her voice fading into the woods. "I'll be fine. There's still light."

CHAPTER 7

Trey looks around at the empty clearing for a second and then follows her into the woods, stopping to gather bark off fallen birch branches. The thin, curly strips are as good as paper when trying to start a fire.

Pockets stuffed, he looks around for Leslie, but she's moved ahead and out of view. "Hey," he yells. "Hey, Leslie! Did you find any dry stuff?" She doesn't answer. "Leslie?"

It's getting darker by the moment in the thick woods, and from far away he can hear the sound of someone chopping wood again. It goes on for just a minute and then stops.

"Leslie," he says again as he follows the trail. No sign of her. He looks through the leaves and ferns and branches for the blue hoodie she was wearing, but he doesn't see it. A gnawing sense of unease flares up in his gut.

"Leslie!" he yells, even louder this time.

Still no answer.

The trail ends at a fallen pine tree. The needles have turned the color of rust—the tree has been dead for a long time. He tests a branch, and it snaps off easily in his hand. Perfect wood for a campfire.

He pulls off a few thin branches from the treetop and then steps off the trail to reach some thicker limbs. His foot lands on a root that rolls under him; he slips and staggers, dropping his armload of wood. He looks down just as the "root" slithers away and disappears into a hole at the base of the fallen tree's trunk.

Snake! I stepped on a snake! He shudders and takes one slow step back, eyes on the hole, and then another, and then something tickles the back of his neck.

"Ahhh!" he cries, jumping up and spinning around and slapping his neck at the same time.

"We're good. I found a bunch of stuff," Leslie says. Her arms are full of branches, including the long, whippy one that brushed his head. He didn't even hear her approach. She laughs. "Scared you?"

He picks up the branches he'd dropped. "I think I just saw a snake," he says, nodding toward the woods.

"I saw one too, I think. I thought it was a tree root, but then it moved."

"Nasty," Trey says. "Same thing happened to me, except I stepped on it, and it disappeared into that hole over there."

Leslie shivers in sympathy, and they start walking back to the campsite. It's getting hard to see the thin path in the evening shade. "Let's get our fire going," she suggests. "Maybe it will keep the slithering creatures away."

"Where were you?" Trey asks a few minutes later. "I was calling your name, and you never answered me."

"I was right over there." She points to another fallen tree.

"I thought maybe you were lost," he says, trying not to sound too relieved as the trail opens again into the campsite.

She drops an armful of tinder next to the fire pit. "I was a Girl Scout for seven years," she says, "and I didn't just sell cookies. My troop and I used to go on two-week wilderness camping trips. You don't have to worry about me and the woods. I can take care of myself."

"So your dad would let you go on wilderness trips, just not here?"

"I know! Weird, right?" She kneels down near the fire pit and makes a small pile of dry leaves, bark, and sticks, then strikes a match and holds it to the leaf layer, gently blowing on the tiny embers. A flame flickers and catches the bark and starts to devour the twigs. Leslie feeds it more sticks and then finally a few large branches.

Trey moves closer to the fire as the larger branches catch. His jeans are still damp, and he hasn't shaken the chill. They watch the fire in silence for a few minutes. Then out of habit, he pulls out his phone.

"Do you have any reception?" he asks.

"I didn't bring my phone," she says.

"Why?"

"My father has this device on it that tracks my every move, and I didn't want him to know I was here, so I pretended like I accidentally left my phone behind on the front porch."

She puts another log on the fire.

"Where does your dad think you are?"

"Camping up at Johnson National Park."

"That's where I wanted to go," Trey says.

"Great fishing," Leslie says, sitting down next to the fire.

Then Trey hears Dominic and Willa. They are laughing as they step back into the campsite, and Trey is suddenly glad that Willa and Leslie came along.

CHAPTER 8

"What's so funny?" Leslie asks as she stands up and steps away from the fire. Willa hands her a long nylon bag, and Leslie loosens the drawstring and shakes the tent and poles out.

"Dominic nearly got run over by a deer," Willa says, still laughing as they spread the tent out across the ground. "It just burst out of the woods and ran in front of him, and Dominic jumped ten feet into the air."

"I thought it was a bear," Dominic says, handing the other tent to Trey. "It was huge."

"It was a fawn," Willa teases.

"Deer have been known to attack people," Dominic says. Trey unrolls his tent, laughing at the image. *Maybe this wasn't such a mistake,* he thinks. It feels good—the laughter, getting away, setting up a tent in the woods with friends and a campfire.

"I'm starving," Willa says when both tents are set up.

"The fire is ready," Leslie says. "I'll get the tofu dogs out."

"Tofu dogs?" Trey says.

"Actually," she says, "they're sun-dried tomato tofu dogs."

"Even better," Trey says, making a face, but he's starving, and he'd eat anything. He gets his camping knife and cuts four skinny, green branches from a poplar tree, shaves off the leaves, and hands everyone a roasting stick.

Leslie passes around the package of tofu dogs. Trey takes one and examines it suspiciously, thinking, *That is a strange shade of pink. Like a hot dog made of bubble gum.*

"You know," Leslie says, "your parents' restaurant would do better if they offered more vegetarian and gluten-free options."

"I'll make sure to tell them that," he responds with an eye roll. His parents run an

Italian restaurant; they make their own pasta and cure their own meat. The dining room is small, but it is usually full, with people waiting at the busiest times. *They could do a lot better if they could afford to expand the place.*

"But I love that all their stuff is fresh and organic," she continues. "Doesn't your mom grow all the herbs herself?"

"Yeah," Trey says. "I've never seen you in the restaurant."

"Our housekeeper picks it up for my dinner," she says.

"It must be nice," Trey says. "Having someone bring you all your meals."

"Actually, it isn't all that nice. I usually end up eating alone in front of my laptop now that my mom is living in California. My parents got divorced a year ago."

"I'm sorry." He looks across the fire at her. "I didn't know."

Trey tries to put the tofu dog on his stick, but it breaks in half and falls in the dirt.

"Here," Leslie says, handing him a new one.

Trey roasts it over the fire, but it doesn't really roast. It just kind of turns a darker shade of pink.

"It's all about the condiments anyhow," Leslie says. She passes around some bean-sprout buns and a bag filled with small bottles of ketchup, mustard, relish, chopped onions, and hot sauce.

Trey puts everything on top of the tofu dog, and when he takes a bite, he's surprised. It's actually pretty good, and he ends up eating four.

CHAPTER 9

The night creeps in around them as they sit by the fire, and a waxing moon slowly rises above the treetops. Leslie throws another log on the fire, and Willa breaks out a bag of marshmallows and passes them around.

"Are these tofu too?" Trey asks, nodding at the bag.

"No." Leslie laughs as she pops one into her mouth. "Pure sugar and cornstarch, but gelatin- and gluten-free, if you were wondering."

"I wasn't," Trey says.

"Tell us about the missing sisters," Willa says as she sits down next to Dominic. "What happened? I'm dying to know."

Trey slowly twirls a marshmallow over the fire, watching it turn from white to a golden brown.

"My dad was there when the first girl went missing," Leslie says. Her skin glows in the orange firelight. "I just found out a month ago. I found this file on his desk at home, and it was filled with newspaper clippings about the college kid who disappeared a year ago. Under those articles were some others about a girl named Louise who disappeared when my dad was in high school. And there was a police report that named my father as a suspect."

"What?" Willa says.

Trey looks at the dark woods behind Leslie. He sees a shadow, but then it is gone. *Just the campfire smoke*, he thinks.

"What happened?" Willa asks leaning closer to the fire.

"My father and Louise and a bunch of kids headed to Lake Helen in the summer of 1984. There were, like, four or five of them—there's a picture of them all standing on the lakeshore. They all look like they were having a good time."

"No vampire flies back then?" Dominic says.

"Shhh," Willa says. "I want to hear the story."

Leslie pokes at the fire with a stick and continues. "That night they all gathered around a campfire on the shore of the lake, and according to the newspaper article, just after midnight, Louise Richards got up and went into the trees for more firewood, and she never came back. Gone. Just like that."

"People don't just disappear," Trey says.

Orange sparks rise up from the crackling fire.

"They searched for her for three days. No sign of her. And after questioning my dad, the other kids, and the family, the sheriff determined that the disappearance was a hoax to cover for Louise running away."

"Why would she run away?" Trey puts another marshmallow on his stick.

"I guess she was really smart and focused on becoming a doctor, but her father was really cruel and told her that he wasn't going to sink money into a girl's education when all she was

42

going to do was end up getting married and having kids."

"No. Way," Willa says. "I'd run away too."

Trey feels for Louise. His parents are great, but part of him wishes he could just take off, leave the family business behind, and do all the things he wants to do. But that's hard without money.

"I know, right?" Leslie says. "Makes sense. Plus, I found letters and notes from Louise to my father. They were in love. They'd dated for over a year, and in her last note she told him she'd gotten some kind of scholarship— enough money to pay for college. She was set. She had the money, she could've gone, but she never claimed the scholarship. She never even showed up to the school."

"So your father thinks someone took her?"

"According to an interview, the day after Louise went missing, my father returned to Lake Helen and set up camp in order to continue searching for her. On the third night, my father heard something just after midnight, and when he went to investigate, he saw a strange man standing at the edge of the woods. Dad tried to question him, tried to ask him who he was, but the man turned away and disappeared."

"Who was he?" Willa says.

"*The Woodsman*—that's what my father wrote under a picture he drew of the man, but the sheriff refused to take him seriously. He was convinced my father helped Louise plan the hoax, but then a year later, Louise's younger sister, Sarah, went to the woods to honor Louise, and she disappeared too."

"What?" Willa says, leaning closer to the fire. "That's crazy."

"I know," Leslie continues. "But the sheriff believed that she ran away to be with Louise. That the two of them started new lives somewhere else."

"Did anyone find evidence of this?" Trey asks. *Strange that three teenagers could just disappear without leaving any trace.*

They are all quiet for a moment, and then Trey turns to Leslie.

"And they never found any clues? Footprints. DNA. Anything?"

"The cases were all closed after the sheriff declared them runaways."

"Wow," Willa says. "That must have broken your dad's heart—having his girlfriend disappear like that."

"It changed him forever," Leslie says. "In his letters, before Louise disappeared, he sounded like such a different person. Gentle. Kind. He wanted to be a teacher." She shakes her head. "I don't think he ever got over her. That's why he never left Middleton. I think he still comes here in secret to search for her." She stares at the fire for a moment. "And I think that's why my parents got a divorce. Louise haunted their marriage."

"That's so sad," Willa says. "I'm sorry."

Leslie throws a stick into the fire. "I've wondered lately what my dad would be like if Louise had never disappeared."

"Maybe he'd be happy," Trey says. "But then you wouldn't be here."

She looks at him. "True, I *wouldn't* be here." She throws him a marshmallow.

"What time is it now?" Dominic says.

"11:11," Willa says, checking her phone and then giving it a shake. "Weird. The battery is nearly dead. I swear it was fully charged before we left, and I haven't even used it."

A sudden breeze stirs the flames.

CHAPTER 10

Willa stands up, stretches her long arms, and looks at all of them.

"How about a game of Truth or Dare?" she asks. "It seems like the perfect night. The perfect setting."

"Really?" Dominic says.

"Really." She rummages through a bag and holds up a blue water bottle. "I'll spin the bottle, and whoever the bottle points to has to either answer a question or do a dare."

She spins the bottle, and it points to Trey. He hesitates and then looks at her. "Truth," he says. He doesn't feel like getting up, and he doesn't want to have to do something stupid.

"Who were your top three high-school crushes?" Willa asks.

Trey feels his face turn red. Suddenly doing a dumb dance or whatever doesn't sound so bad. "Um . . . " He swallows. "Toni Evans, freshman year," he admits. *Safe enough, she moved to Salt Lake City two years ago, so she'll never find out.*

"Two more! Did you ever have a crush on Leslie?" Willa teases him.

Everyone stares at him.

"I never really knew her before."

"You never liked me—admit it," she says.

"It wasn't you," Trey finally says. "I just never liked how your father treated my parents. He's been a tough landlord."

"He's so focused on money," Leslie says. "I'm sorry."

Trey looks across the fire at her. "But you're not like him. Not at all. You're really nice and funny, and I wish we would've known each other better a long time ago."

"Aw, Trey, you're off the hook with two crushes. This is better than therapy!" Willa crows. She spins the bottle again. This time it points at Leslie.

"Truth or dare?"

"Truth," Leslie says.

Willa looks at her, thinking.

"I know," Dominic interrupts, leaning forward, "do you think your dad had anything to do with Louise's disappearance?"

"No," Leslie says. "No. Way."

"Are you positive?"

Leslie looks a bit shaken. "I know he can be cold and calculating and controlling, but he's not evil. He'd never hurt anyone."

Clouds move across the moon, and it suddenly seems darker than before.

"Of course he didn't have anything to do with her disappearance," Willa says, touching Leslie's back. "Why would you ask that?"

Willa sits back down and spins the bottle again. This time it points to her.

"Truth," Willa says, but then she shakes her head and jumps up. "No. I'm going to mix this up and take a dare instead. And to be truthful, I've never done anything really daring. Not once. Everything I've done has been safe. Good grades. Smart choices. So, I'm going to dare *myself* to do something . . . I'm going to dare myself to enter the woods and stay there until after midnight." And with that, she suddenly laughs, turns, and sprints into the woods.

"Willa!" Leslie calls after her. But Willa disappears into the darkness before any of them can even stand up.

"Not funny," Dominic says as they walk toward the line of trees after Willa.

"Willa? Answer us!"

"I'm fine," they hear her say. She's not far away, but they can't see her in the darkness. "I just want to make it until after midnight. I can do this."

"Don't go any farther," Trey says. "You'll get lost." He grabs a flashlight out of his backpack and shines it into the woods.

"Come on," Leslie says. "This is dumb. Please come back to the fire."

They listen for Willa's answer, but the woods are silent except for the crackling fire.

Then, "What time is it?" Willa asks. Her voice is coming from another location. She seems to be farther away.

"Willa?" Dominic says. "Seriously. Not funny. Not funny at all."

Trey looks down at his phone. It is nearly midnight.

"Come out," Trey says.

"Not until after midnight."

Something moves through the forest. They hear breaking branches and then, from far away, a muffled scream.

"Willa?" Dominic yells, already running into the woods.

Trey shines his light into the forest, and he and Leslie follow, all three of them calling Willa's name.

CHAPTER 11

"We have to find her!" Dominic yells. Branches and tree roots grab at their arms and legs. Trey tries to shine his light up ahead, but thick underbrush blocks the light after only a few feet.

"This way," Trey calls. His flashlight shines on a figure moving quickly through the forest. "Willa!" he yells, though he knows it isn't Willa—the shoulders are too wide, the arms are too long. It looks more like the Woodsman.

"Did you see her?" Leslie says.

"I saw someone," Trey says.

"Shhh," Dominic says. "We need to stop and listen for her."

The three of them freeze, but they can only hear the sound of their breath and their beating hearts.

"Willa!" Dominic yells again. "Say something. Make a sound."

But there is nothing. It is as if she has just disappeared, and then Trey's flashlight glints off something hanging from a tree branch. It's Willa's silver bracelet, still swinging back and forth, as if it just fell from her wrist.

Dominic takes the bracelet from Trey.

"I gave her that for her birthday," he says.

Leslie declares, "I should've never let us come here. I should've listened to my father. He knew. He knew!"

Trey tries his phone again, but there's no reception. "We have to get help," he says.

"We aren't leaving her. Not alone," Dominic says.

Just then they hear a muffled, faraway scream.

"This way," Leslie shouts, leading the way. They move as fast as they can, deeper into the woods, but Trey's flashlight only illuminates a narrow path.

They stop to listen again, and the flashlight flickers and goes out. Trey looks around, blinking in the sudden darkness, and realizes they are lost. There is no sign of their campfire, not even a whiff of smoke. He has no idea what direction to go.

Dominic checks his phone and turns it off almost immediately. "No reception. And my battery is really low," he mutters.

"Mine too," Trey says, almost whispering. "We need at least one phone. So shut yours down and I'll use mine as a light, and maybe if we get to higher ground, we'll get some reception and be able to call for help."

"Do you have a compass on your phone?" Leslie says. "We need to follow a straight line or we'll just end up going in circles."

Trey opens the compass application. "It doesn't work," he says, "the arrow just spins around and around."

"We have to keep searching," Dominic says, moving between trees.

"But we don't even know which way to go," Trey says.

From even deeper in the forest, all of three of them hear the sound of someone chopping wood again. *Chop. Chop. Chop.* Slow and steady.

"This way," Leslie says, and Trey and Dominic follow her. They don't know what else to do. They move through the forest, trying to follow the sound, but after a few moments the chopping stops, and it is quiet again.

CHAPTER 12

They've walked for nearly an hour. Trey leans against a tree, rubbing a deep scratch on his arm from a tree branch, and looks up at the dark, cloudy sky. He can't even find a star to follow.

"What are we going to do?" Trey says.

"Look," Leslie says, pointing through the trees. "Do you see it? That silvery light?"

Dominic squints. Trey follows her finger and spots a sliver of light. It is far away, but it is there.

"We need to walk straight toward it," Leslie says. "Try not to blink, or we'll lose it."

They push slowly forward, eyes on the silver trickle of light. Trey hears something, the babbling of a creek somewhere close, but where? Suddenly Leslie trips, and Trey catches her arm.

"Thanks," she says, sounding shaken. "There's a drop-off there—the ground just went out from under my foot. If you hadn't caught me . . . "

Trey raises his phone, and the dim light shows that they have been moving along a ravine that now curves across their path. As they back away, something slithers across leaves in the darkness.

"Snake!" they hear Dominic hiss.

"Look out!" they call, but it's too late. Dominic shouts once as he goes over the edge of the ravine, crashing through the brush into the darkness below.

"Dominic!" Trey yells, shining his dying phone down into the ravine. "Are you okay?"

"Oh man," Dominic says, sounding strained. "I think I broke my arm."

"Turn your phone on so we can see the light."

"I don't know where it is. I can't see it anywhere . . . and my arm. It really hurts."

"We're coming down," Trey says. "Don't move. Just keep talking."

"I'm just going to count," Dominic says in a weak voice. "One . . . two . . . three . . . four . . . five . . . six . . . "

The dirt is loose and rocky. Trey and Leslie slip and slide toward Dominic's voice, but as they reach flatter ground, he stops counting.

"Dominic?" Trey shouts. "Keep counting. Keep talking."

There is no response.

"Dominic? Say something, please!" Leslie pleads.

Trey and Leslie stop and listen, but all they hear is the sound of something being dragged through the woods.

"Dominic!"

No answer.

"The Woodsman has Dominic too," Trey says, shining his phone in the direction of the sound.

"Put it away! Turn it off," Leslie says, "or the Woodsman will see us and we'll be next."

They crouch behind a tree, staring into the darkness, but they can't see anything and there is no sound other than the running creek.

"Look," Leslie says. She points to a twinkling light now not very far away.

CHAPTER 13

The light grows brighter until Trey and Leslie step out past a ring of felled trees into a small clearing. In the middle is a wooden shack. The light is coming through a rip in the curtain that covers the window.

"He must have taken them here," Trey whispers as they quietly approach the structure.

"We need a plan to get them out."

"First we need to get a look inside," Trey says. He's afraid of what he'll see, but he has to find out what happened to his friends.

As quietly as they can, they move to the back of the shack. There are no other windows or doors. From inside they hear movement and then a grinding sound. They freeze and listen, trying not to breathe.

Trey finds a crack in the wall, covered with a piece of tar paper. He peels it back and peers inside, and he slides his other hand over his mouth to stifle a gasp. The Woodsman is right there! He's rocking in a chair, sharpening the blade of an ax, and on the ground in front of him, unmoving and limp, are Willa and Dominic. At first he thinks they are dead, but then Dominic opens his eyes and gives Willa a terrified look, and Willa opens her eyes and returns it.

The Woodsman rhythmically slides a dark stone against the silvery blade of his ax. *Rasp, rasp, rasp*, the stone slides along, and on the third stroke the Woodsman's green and amber eyes—the ranger's strange eyes—look up from his ax and directly into Trey's.

"Run," Trey whispers to Leslie. "He saw me. Go. Hide yourself. Now."

Leslie takes off and hides behind a woodpile as Trey tries to grab his pocketknife, but a slithering black thing grabs it from his hand. Then something loops around his wrist, and another "something" snares his foot so he can't run—he can't even move.

"Another one," the ranger says as he comes out, sounding pleased.

"Who are you?" Trey says as the man pulls something out of the pocket of his worn jeans—a red leaf.

"I am the Woodsman," the man says. He puts the leaf over Trey's mouth, and though Trey shakes his head, he can't get away. When the leaf touches his lips, Trey loses his voice and all his strength. He looks up at the man standing above him.

"Yes, I will feed you soon," the Woodsman says, and Trey realizes he is speaking to the trees rising up behind the shack. The Woodsman grabs Trey's shirt, and suddenly his arms and legs are free and the things that grabbed him are wiggling back along the ground. *Those aren't snakes. They're the roots of the trees!*

The Woodsman drags Trey into the shack. It takes every ounce of Trey's remaining strength, but he turns his head just enough to scrape the leaf off of his mouth. With the leaf gone, he can speak again.

"What do you want?" he rasps. His arms and legs are still floppy and weak.

"It isn't what *I* want," the Woodsman says. "It is what the trees want."

"What are you talking about?" Trey says.

"It is time to go. Now get up. UP!" The Woodsman rips the red leaves off of Willa and Dominic's mouths. "The trees have tasted you, and they will feed on you. Such bright minds. Such youth. They will consume you and bloom."

Pain twists Dominic's face as he stands up—his broken arm is twisted at a weird angle behind his back, and his face is white.

"Now march," the Woodsman says, holding his ax across his chest with one hand and pushing the three of them out the door with the other. They stumble on shaky legs in the darkness, falling and taking one another down.

"Get up. Get up," the Woodsman says.

"Hurry. The bloom is near, and the trees must be fed. They told me it is time. It is time. The moon will be full tomorrow night. Go."

"What did you do to the other kids?" Trey asks.

"Silence!" The Woodsman flings his ax at Trey. He flinches but the ax whirs over his head like the blades of a helicopter and then returns to the Woodsman's hand. Trey's knees turn to jelly and he falls to the ground.

The Woodsman purrs, "You will soon see the others."

"Don't mess with him," Willa whispers as Trey gets back up. But he's not listening, because out of the corner of his eye he sees a figure duck behind a tree. Leslie is following them.

Yes! We're saved! he thinks—but then, *No! She'll be captured too, and then we all die!*

The Woodsman herds them toward the grove behind the shack. The moon slides out from behind the clouds, and Trey realizes has never seen such trees in his life. The moonlight glints off silver and amber scales, and roots writhe and entwine at the base of the trunks. Trey shudders when he sees that the trunks pulse and swallow like long, narrow throats.

A slight breeze blows, and at the top of the tree, tiny silver pods move and click together with a sound like chattering teeth.

"Listen," the Woodsman says as he stares up at the branches. "The trees are pleased. It has been thirty years, but the trees have borne fruit, and inside are the seeds of the future."

"What future?" Trey says.

"Silence!" the Woodsman commands. He reaches down towards the moss-covered ground and pulls open a hidden door. He forces the three of them down a steep wooden staircase made of black roots that twists and turns, leading them deeper and deeper into the earth. Glowing silver crystals embedded in the walls light the way.

The stairs end at a wooden door. The Woodsman shoves them forward and presses his hand against it, and the door opens, spilling the three of them into a chilly cavern. It smells of earth and something sweet. The door shuts behind them, and Trey sees three hollowed-out tree trunks lying on the ground like coffins.

The Woodsman pushes them all forward, and Trey sees that each trunk contains a young person suspended in a thick amber liquid. One boy and two girls. The ends of the black roots dangle in the liquid, and Trey realizes that they are feeding the trees above.

CHAPTER 14

"You will make my Saturian trees so happy," the Woodsman says as the black roots carry two more tree-trunk coffins into the room and set them near the wall. The ax marks on the trunks are still fresh: the chopping sound was the Woodsman cutting these trees and carving out coffins—for them.

"Saturian trees?" Trey says.

"Yes," the Woodsman says proudly. "Soon, they will take over the earth. Once the trees have fed, the silver pods will burst open and their seeds will spread across the earth. They will grow and flourish, fed by the entire human race."

Willa looks at him. "Why? Why do you want to destroy our world?"

"Destroy it? Humans destroy it themselves. The trees will save Earth. They will keep humans from hurting this world any more."

Trey tries to bolt for the door, but black, slithering roots pull tight around his ankles.

"Let us go!" he yells at the Woodsman.

"Oh no," the Woodsman says. "The trees need fresh minds in order to bloom."

The Woodsman waves a hand, and the roots drag Trey across the dirt floor to one of the tree coffins. Inside it, Trey sees a blond-haired boy suspended in amber liquid. The boy opens his eyes, and his right hand moves, as if reaching for the surface.

"They're alive," Trey yells to Dominic and Willa.

"Of course they are," says the Woodsman. "They are kept dreaming in order to feed the trees."

The boy mouths the word, "Help," then closes his eyes again.

CHAPTER 15

Thick, twisting roots slither around Trey's face like tongues.

"Not yet. Not yet," the Woodsman says, pushing the roots away with the handle of his ax. "Remember, we must let the humans ferment."

The roots retreat.

"You," he says to Willa, pushing her toward one of the new tree trunks. "Get in. So bright and strong. You will feed the trees well."

Willa pulls away as Dominic lunges forward, yelling, "Let her go!" But roots whip out and pin him to the ground.

"No," the Woodsman responds. "This is what the trees require."

The woodsman twists a copper spigot on the wall, and a syrupy liquid flows into the first new tree trunk. The stream is hypnotizing as it slowly fills up the emptiness.

"Get in," the Woodsman demands again, but Willa kicks and elbows him. The ax clatters to the ground as the Woodsman tries to slap another leaf over Willa's mouth. Then the door crashes open, and Leslie tumbles into the cavern, grabs the ax, and waves it wildly above her head.

Startled, the Woodsman turns to Leslie, and Willa throws her shoulder into his side and topples him into the amber liquid before slapping a red leaf across his mouth. His eyes bulge, but his limbs only twitch, and the black roots rasp against the floor in their slithering haste to drink.

Leslie chops through the vines pinning Trey and Dominic to the ground. The severed roots scream in high-pitched whistles, and amber liquid oozes out onto the floor.

"Let's get out of here. Now!" she shouts, but Trey is heading across the room to where the three kids float in amber liquid. The closest holds a girl in a bright-pink, oversized sweatshirt and jeans. Her curly black hair is pulled up into a matching pink scrunchie.

"We can't leave them," he says. "They're still alive. We have to get them out of here!"

He reaches into the amber liquid, but it is like putting his hands into quicksand. He can't reach the girl, and he can't pull his arms out.

"How do we stop it?" Leslie says.

Willa points to the roots feeding on the liquid, and Leslie brings the ax down on the thickest cluster of them. The room vibrates with shrill tree screams.

"Keep going!" Trey gets his hands under the girl's arms and pulls her into a sitting position. She gasps air and coughs out strings of amber syrup. "I think the roots create a suction of some kind," he yells as he hauls her over the edge.

Leslie chops her way through the roots, and Trey follows her, pulling the next girl free and then the boy. Dominic is crouched down, speaking to the first girl, and then he helps her up with his good arm.

"Can you walk?" Trey asks the boy, who is still coughing.

"They have to do better than that," Leslie warns as black roots slither toward their legs. "They have to run!"

The missing teens move slowly, as if they aren't used to Earth's gravity, and Trey, Willa, and Dominic are still woozy from the red leaves. Still, they make it through the door, Leslie slicing any root that gets too close, and when it slams shut behind them it shudders under the pounding of a hundred wooden fists.

CHAPTER 16

When they reach the top of the steps, they start to head into the woods—but Trey shouts, "Wait! Leslie! We have to cut the trees down! We can't let them bloom. They'll feed off every human on Earth. Willa, Dominic, you keep running with the other three."

The ground shivers as roots, hundreds of them, slither in, grabbing at ankles and legs. Leslie cuts herself free with the ax and then slices at the roots tangling around the others' legs. Willa leads the other four past the shack as Trey and Leslie head deeper into the grove of scaly trees.

"Go for the trunks," Trey pants. The trees shake, and red leaves and silver blossoms fall all around them. "Don't let the leaves touch your face!"

Leslie swings the ax as hard as she can at the closest tree. It hits not with the sound of metal against wood, but with the squelch of something soft. The tree screeches as thick amber liquid pours onto the ground.

"Timber!" Trey yells as the tree crumples and falls.

Leslie is already swinging at the next trunk, and the keening of dying trees is deafening. Red leaves flutter around them, sticking to their skin and hair. The last of the trunks collapses, and Trey and Leslie peel leaves off as fast as they can and run for the woods, where the non-alien trees seem to be reaching out, as if offering safety.

Soon they catch up with the others. "This way," Leslie says, pointing to the east, where the sky is starting to turn from indigo to a light violet. "We just need to keep moving toward the rising sun, and sooner or later, we'll find our way out."

As they walk, Leslie turns to the tall girl in the pink sweatshirt.

"Are you Louise?" she asks.

She nods.

"I'm Andrew Miller's daughter," she says.

The girl stops in her tracks, and a tear escapes from her eye.

"How long have I been gone?" she whispers.

"A long time," Leslie says.

"This my sister, Sarah," she says as the other girl reaches for her hand. Her hair is tied into a side ponytail, and she looks a lot like Louise. "She came to search for me, and the Woodsman took her too."

"And you are Sasha?" Trey asks the thin, blond boy.

"Yes," he says.

"Your parents have been searching for you."

"I've been dreaming of going home. I wish I would've never left." He has a thick Russian accent.

"We will get you all back home," Trey declares.

As they make their way through the woods, the sun rises higher, turning the woods into a spectacle of shimmering golden light.

CHAPTER 17

They stop at a stream to drink. Then Louise, Sarah, and Sasha wade in to wash the thick, sticky liquid from their skin. As they do, Louise and Sarah rapidly age. Gray streaks appear in their hair, and their bodies lose their youth.

"What is happening?" Louise asks, looking at her wrinkling hands.

"We need to keep going," Trey says, taking her arm. "We need to get you to safety. You've been gone for a long time."

The seven of them walk through the forest for nearly three hours, jumping nervously with every cracked twig. At the top of a steep, rocky incline, Trey says, "Everyone check your phones. See if you have reception."

"You're the only one left with a phone," Dominic reminds him.

"Phones?" Louise says. "You carry them with you?"

Trey shows her his phone. "A lot has changed since 1984."

"Crazy," Louise says, watching the screen light up.

"One bar," Trey says. He tries to make a call, but it drops. He puts his phone back in his pocket and they continue on.

An hour later, just as the sun is starting to come up, they find a trail; as it crests a hill, they see the ranger station and Lake Helen below.

"We made it!" Leslie says as they step into the clearing. But behind them comes the sound of branches breaking beneath heavy, running feet. Trey knows before turning around that it is the Woodsman.

CHAPTER 18

The Woodsman steps out of the woods. Amber syrup covers his skin, and he glistens in the sun.

"Get to the car," Trey says. Leslie hands him the ax, but a strong force seizes it from his hands, and it flies through the air to the Woodsman's hands.

"Go," Trey yells to the others. "Run."

The Woodsman swings the ax, growling, "You destroyed my trees. You destroyed the new future of this world."

"Who gave you the seeds? How did you get them?" Trey says, trying to buy the others time.

The Woodsman looks not only angry, but anguished. "They were sent to me," he says.

"Who sent them?" Trey asks. *If I keep him talking, the others have a better chance of getting to the car.*

"Years ago, a meteorite crashed on the shore of Lake Helen, and when I went to investigate, I found a silver pod filled with seeds. As soon as I touched them, I knew their power. I knew what to do. They spoke to me. They told me what needed to be done. Years I have taken care of those trees. Years."

"And they told you they were sent here to take over the Earth?" Trey says.

"To take over the human race," the Woodsman says. "The trees knew the value of this world; humans do not."

"Most of us want to make the world a better place," Trey says.

The Woodsman steps closer to him. Trey backs away.

"You could help me," the Woodsman says, pulling a silver pod out of his pocket. "Just hold this in your hand. Feel the energy. You could help me care for the new trees. I will not give up. I will start again."

A fly circles Trey's head and then another and another, and suddenly a swarm descends upon the Woodsman, covering his syrupy face and arms.

Trey bolts down the path and catches up to the others at the car. "We need to get out of here."

Dominic throws Trey the keys. "You drive. I won't be able to steer with my arm."

"He's coming!" Leslie yells as Dominic, Willa, and the three missing kids cram into the backseat. The fly-covered Woodsman stumbles down the hill toward them.

"You're my copilot," Trey says to Leslie. "You keep your eyes on the Woodsman, and I'll keep my eyes on the road."

"Hurry!" Leslie says, looking out the rear window. But when Trey turns the key, the engine sputters and dies.

"Try it again, and don't flood the engine," Dominic says from behind him.

Trey turns the key again and steps lightly on the gas. The engine turns over, and he jerks the car into gear just as the Woodsman's ax slams against the trunk.

"Go!" Leslie shouts as the Woodsman pulls the ax out of the car.

Trey guns it up the road, swerving left and right as the Woodsman chases them, but slowly he loses ground.

Trey throws his phone to Leslie.

"When you see even one bar, dial 9-1-1."

They approach the fallen tree blocking the road.

"We're trapped," Dominic says, looking out the back window. The Woodsman is still following them, his ax raised above his head.

"We made it past this tree once. We can do it again," Trey says. He yanks the steering wheel around with all of his might and shouts, "Hold on!" as the car dives into the ditch. The car ricochets off a rock near the bottom and Willa, crammed in on one side, cries out as her head hits the window. Trey steps on the gas, and the car surges up the steep bank and back onto the road.

They gain only a few hundred feet before the ax strikes the back tire.

"Keep going!" Dominic yells, but the ax jams against the wheel well and the engine revs uselessly. Leslie throws open the door, jumps out, and pries the ax out of the tire.

"Pop the trunk," she yells as she throws Dominic the phone.

Trey pulls a lever, and Leslie drops the ax in the cooler, locks it, and slams the trunk closed.

"Nice," Trey says as she hops back in the car.

They keep going even though the back tire is flat and the metal rim strikes sparks against the gravel.

"I got 9-1-1! There's a sheriff in the area already!" Dominic shouts, holding the phone up for all to see. "What do I tell them?"

"Tell them to hurry!" Trey says.

The car thunks down the road. Everyone cheers as the trees thin out, revealing the flashing of red and blue lights turning off the highway onto the road ahead.

CHAPTER 19

As the sheriff's car stops in front of them on the narrow road, Leslie takes the phone from Dominic to call her dad. A short but strong-looking uniformed man gets out of the car and storms over to the driver's-side window.

"What's going on here?" the sheriff asks, looking suspiciously into their packed, muddy car.

"The Woodsman," Trey says. It comes out all wobbly. Adrenalin is coursing through his veins.

"The Woodsman," Leslie says into the phone to her dad.

"We found the missing kids," they both say at the same time.

"I don't understand," the sheriff says and then nods to Leslie. "Put the phone down."

The back window rolls down. "I'm Louise," she says. "I've been missing since 1984. My sister and I were kidnapped."

The sheriff shakes his head. "What kind of prank are you all pulling?" he asks.

"We aren't making this up," Leslie says. "My dad is on his way. Andrew Miller. He'll explain everything."

"There's a madman and he calls himself the Woodsman and he's been growing alien trees—"

"I don't believe any of this," the sheriff says. "Do you know the penalty for pranking 9-1-1?" As he steps away from their car, though, the Woodsman appears behind them on the road, still surrounded by a swarm of black flies.

"There he is!" Trey yells to the sheriff. "He's coming for us!"

The sheriff takes one look at the Woodsman and puts his hand on his gun.

"Stop where you are!" he commands.

"You will pay," the Woodsman says. "My trees, my trees!"

"Who are you?" The gun is in the sheriff's hand.

"I am the Woodsman—keeper of the Saturian trees."

He releases a flurry of red leaves in the sheriff's face, and the short man crumples to the ground.

The Woodsman opens his right hand, and a banging noise from the trunk shakes the car. *Bang. Bang. Bang.* The ax slices through the cooler and then through the lock on the trunk to fly back into the Woodsman's hand.

"You will all come with me now," the Woodsman says, holding the ax in one hand and taking a silver pod out of his pocket with the other. "All is not lost. You all will help me replant my trees, and you will help them grow. Together we will start again."

Trey looks for something, anything, to help them escape. But then Louise gets out and stalks toward the Woodsman, shouting, "You have taken years of my life. You have taken our youth." A confused look crosses the Woodsman's face as she points to her sister and Sasha. "We. Will. Not. Go. With. You."

She leaps, fast and furious, ducking when he swings the ax and then tackling him to the ground. She smacks a red leaf over his mouth and nose. His eyes go wide, but the ax falls from suddenly powerless fingers.

"You are no longer the Woodsman," she says, standing over his limp form. "You are just a man who will soon go to jail. You will pay for every minute you stole from us."

The rest of them jump out of the car. Sarah is hugging Louise, and Willa is peeling the leaf off the sheriff's face. Leslie picks up the ax and stands guard over the Woodsman. Trey looks down at the Woodsman and realizes that his left fist is still clenched. When Trey gingerly pries the Woodsman's fingers apart, three silver pods roll out. Trey catches them before they can hit the ground, and their power crackles across his palm like electricity.

Promise, such promise! They speak directly to his mind, so pleased, so excited, so tempting.

You alone hold the power to save Earth. Serve us, and we will reward you beyond your wildest dreams!

For a moment he can almost see it: an end to extinctions and deforestation and drought, to hunger and inequality. *All will be healthy and happy with us*, the voices promise. But he has seen the aliens' plan, and behind their promises he sees all humanity helpless and enslaved, sucked dry as the trees displace all other living things from the planet.

"I *am* saving Earth," he mutters, but the seeds seem to be feeding on his every thought. Suddenly all three pods pop open, and three tiny, snakelike creatures escape and slither across the ground.

"Catch them!" Trey yells as the creatures start to burrow into the dirt. He catches one, and it twists so hard around his finger that it turns blue. It feels like a leech, sucking all his thoughts out of his mind. He digs his nails into its scaly sides, and it screeches and lets go. He throws it to the ground and stomps on it. "Keep it there!" Leslie calls, and then she's beside him, kneeling down, slicing the tiny thing into pieces with the ax. It twitches a few times and is still, and then the thing dissolves into a horrible-smelling slime.

"Do you think there are more pods?" Trey says to Leslie.

"I don't know. I got the other two things though." She holds the ax firmly in her hands. Trey looks around. Willa and Louise have bound the Woodsman's hands and feet with duct tape they found under a seat in the car, and Sarah seems to be working on a splint for Dominic's arm.

Then the sound of shrieking tires splits the air as a white BMW turns the corner into the park, followed by four police cruisers.

"That's my dad," Leslie says faintly.

The BMW pulls up behind the sheriff's car, and Leslie's dad is out the door before the engine dies. "I told you to never come here," he says, sounding angry but hugging her tight. Seven police officers, one with a dog, split up between the dazed sheriff and the trussed Woodsman. "Do you understand now? Do you understand why I never wanted you to come here?"

"I'm sorry," Leslie says. "I'm so sorry."

Louise steps forward. "Andrew, your daughter and her friends saved us," she says, gesturing at Sarah and Sasha. "They freed us all."

"Louise?" Mr. Miller says, stepping closer and gently touching her face.

"Yes," Louise says. She reaches out to him.

"I searched and searched for you. I never gave up." He pulls her into a tight embrace.

"I dreamed for years that you would find me," Louise says. "And you did. You created a daughter who is fearless, who fought for us."

Mr. Miller's hard face softens. He turns back to Leslie and hugs her again. "You did something I was unable to do—you found my friend. You saved her. Thank you."

Trey watches with a smile, but something tugs at his thoughts. *What if there are more silver pods—more seeds, more slithering roots ready to take hold in the earth?*

He tries to explain everything to one of the officers, but they don't believe him until Leslie steps up next to him, a red leaf in her hand.

"This is how I was kidnapped," she says to one of the officers. "Here, smell it." He rolls his eyes, but when he sniffs, the leaf attaches and he falls to the ground.

She quickly tears it off, and another officer makes a phone call—evidently to someone important, because in less than hour, a convoy of three black SUVs flies down the highway and surrounds them all.

CHAPTER 20

Six people—four men and two women—in dark suits and sunglasses get out of the first two black SUVs. Two head straight for Trey and Leslie.

"What are we going to say?" Leslie asks.

"I don't know," Trey admits. "But they need to know there might be more pods."

"We need to show them the cavern too," Leslie says. "Who knows what else is down there."

The black-clad crew approaches, and Trey and Leslie take turns telling them about the Woodsman and the trees.

"You need to show us where these trees grew," a woman with pale skin and dark hair says to them.

Trey looks over at Dominic and Willa, who are talking to two other agents outside an ambulance, and then he sees Louise, Sarah, and Sasha being ushered into one of the SUVs by another agent.

"Where are they going?" Trey asks the woman in black.

"We are going to have a doctor check them all out. How are you doing?"

She looks at Trey and then at Leslie.

"Fine, I think," Trey says.

"Good," she says. "We need you to show us these trees."

Leslie's father is there in a second, saying, "I'm not letting my daughter enter those woods without me."

Soon Trey and Leslie are retracing their steps to the campsite with Mr. Miller, two special agents, two police officers, and the police dog in tow. The fire has gone out, the tents are still standing, and a bag of marshmallows is sitting on the ground, now attracting ants.

"We were sitting here," Trey says, picking up the bag and popping an ant-free marshmallow into his mouth. "And then we ran over here somewhere to follow Willa."

The police dog, a German shepherd, sniffs the ground and leads them down into the ravine. What seemed like hours of travel in the dark turned out to be barely a mile straight through the trees. As they approach the shack, the dog freezes and begins to growl. The breeze picks up, and the scent of rot fills the air.

Hundreds of angry, black flies buzz around where the trees once stood. As they swoop down on the humans, the woman in black catches one in her hand, pulls out a plastic bag, and zips it inside.

"Interesting," she says.

She nods at the other agent, who takes a small silver canister from a pocket inside his dress jacket, pushes a button, and sets it on the ground. As he steps away, the canister begins to flash blue, and the flies head for the light. With a crackle and zap, the light incinerates them.

"Don't go near that," the agent says, nodding at the light, but Leslie and Trey have already backed away.

"They should totally sell that in camping stores," Trey says.

"Too dangerous," the agent says.

The officers move to where the trees once stood, and Trey warns, "Don't touch the red leaves!" But when they get closer, he sees that the leaves have turned crisp and dry, and when he steps on one, it turns to dust.

"Look for silver pods," Leslie says as they walk around the grove. Everyone looks down, but the pods they find have shriveled up, and inside the seeds have turned to goo.

One of the officers and both agents descend into the cavern, flashlights shining, guns drawn. Trey and Leslie wait off to the side.

"Look," Trey says. A few feet away, the sun glints off something hanging from the branch of a pine tree. The two of them slowly walk toward the silver light.

Two silver pods are hanging just a few feet above their heads. They are open, and whatever was inside of them is now gone. Trey has a horrible feeling that somewhere in the woods, another alien tree will take root.

CHAPTER 21

The next day, there is no parade, no story on the front page of the paper. Everything has been classified as Top Secret. Trey and his friends, and their parents, have signed papers and sworn never to talk about the alien trees or possessed rangers or empty silver pods.

"We don't want mass hysteria," the lead agent explained. "For the sake of our nation, you must keep this quiet until a full investigation is complete."

Everyone has gathered at the Millers' house to meet Sasha's parents, who flew in from Russia on the first available flight. They embrace Trey, Leslie, Dominic, and Willa in turn.

"Thank you," Sasha's mother says. "Thank you for returning our son to us."

"My father and mother wish for you to have these," Sasha says, handing each of them a red envelope.

"It will never be enough," Sasha's father says, "but it is a token of our great gratitude."

Trey opens his first. Inside is a check for a hundred thousand dollars. He looks at Dominic, Willa, and Leslie, who are all are wide-eyed too.

"Thank you," Trey says to Sasha's parents. Sasha's father wraps him in another bear-like hug.

"It is the reward money," Sasha's mother says. "And we reward you."

When Trey is released from the hug, he turns and looks at his friends. "Who's up for another camping trip?"

They all raise their hands.

Trey has a lot of phone calls to make, and some packing to do. But in a year, they will meet again at Lake Helen. And they won't be just camping: they will be searching for any sign of sprouting alien trees, searching for slithering black roots.

ABOUT THE AUTHOR

K. R. Coleman is a writer and teacher. She loves teaching students how to tell a scary story at the Loft Literary Center. Her writing has been published in *Crab Orchard Review*, *Paper Darts*, *McSweeney's Internet Tendencies*, *Canvas*, and *Revolver*. She is a recent winner of the 2014–2015 Loft Mentor Series and Minnesota Emerging Writers' Grant. She lives in South Minneapolis with her husband, two boys, and a dog named Happy.